Babar characters TM & © 1990 L. de Brunhoff
All rights reserved.
Based on the animated series "Babar"
A Nelvana-Ellipse Presentation
a Nelvana Production in Association with The Clifford Ross Company, Ltd

Based on characters created
by Jean and Laurent de Brunhoff

Image adaptation by Van Gool-Lefèvre-Loiseaux
Produced by Twin Books U.K. Ltd, London

This 1990 edition published by JellyBean Press,
distributed by Outlet Book Company, Inc.,
A Random House Company, 225 Park Avenue South,
New York, New York 10003

ISBN 0-517-05212-1

8 7 6 5 4 3 2 1
Printed in Italy

BABAR

and His Friends

In the Forest

Twin Books

JellyBean Press
New York

"Let's spend the day in the forest," says Babar, as he closes up his heavy  . "It's so pretty and pleasant there in the fall."

"Oh, yes!" says Pom. I'll take my  ."

"What a funny idea," says Alexander. "Why don't you take along your  ? It's useful."

"Do you think there will be wolves there?" Arthur asks the Old Lady, taking a wicker  .

"Of course not," she replies. "Don't worry about it."

Flora wants her  , and Celeste is helping her put them on. Soon they will be ready to start.

backpack,
harmonica,
pocketknife,
basket, boots

Babar guides his little band along the road,

tapping with his long  to set the pace.

Celeste walks just behind him. To prevent them

all from getting lost, she has brought a  .

"Hurry up, Zephir," says Pom. "Don't dawdle.

And please pass me the  . I'm thirsty."

Arthur wants to imitate Babar and has found a

forked  to use as a walking stick. "Hey!

Wait for me!" calls Alexander, running to catch up.

"Where were you?" asks the Old Lady. "I almost

left behind my ," he answers.

walking stick,
compass,
canteen,
branch,
jacket

Babar has stopped in front of the oldest  in the forest. He points it out to the

others, but Alexander doesn't listen: He is too busy

laughing. "Do you all see this ? It looks

just like Zephir. It's even wearing the same beret!"

"Don't go near this  , Pom," advises the

Old Lady. "It's poisonous! However, you can pick

that mushroom with the yellow  on

it. It may not be very pretty, but it won't hurt you."

Flora has tried to pick a ripe , but the

bush has thorns on it. Celeste will help her.

oak tree,
acorn,
mushroom,
slug,
berry

The hikers have stopped for a little rest.

"The forest is so beautiful," exclaims Celeste.

"Just look at the color of this fallen  !"

Zephir wants to play a game of tag, but Pom is

more interested in the slender green

Alexander has made him from a willow branch.

"May I shoot just one  ?" he asks.

Babar and Arthur are building a hut together.

"Look, I can put one more  on the roof,"

says Arthur proudly. "Do you see, Flora?"

But Flora would rather look at her  .

leaf, bow,
arrow,
fern,
thistle

The children have walked deeper into the forest.

Zephir sees a brown  on the branch of a

chestnut tree and tries to follow it through the

trees. "Wait for me!" he cries. "Don't go so fast!"

Alexander offers a ripe to the little animal,

but he is too late. The squirrel has already gone.

Pom tries to take a tasty out of its

burr. "Ouch!" he yells, "it's sticking me!"

"You could break it open with your ," says

Arthur. Then he calls, "Hey, everyone. Look at

this hungry  in my chestnut!"

squirrel,
nut,
chestnut,
shoe,
caterpillar

Suddenly, a clearing in the woods opens before

them, and they see a  made of logs.

"I would think no one lived out here," says Arthur.

"See! A  on the porch," exclaims Alexander.

"Don't go too near the house, children," warns the

Old Lady. "It's not polite to trespass."

"I'd like to try on those little  ," says Flora.

Babar and Celeste wait for the others by the fence,

and a  watches the noisy strangers in the

yard. They don't see him perched quietly on a bush

of at the edge of the clearing.

cabin,
rocking chair,
wooden shoes,
robin,
holly

Walking around the little house, the children

discover a sharp  and a big woodpile.

"This must be the home of a woodcutter," explains

Arthur, who has also spotted a  .

"The robin seems to be quite tame," says Flora. "He's

showing us his master's  on the ledge."

"It's too hard, Alexander," says Pom, as they try to

saw through a  . "I wish we'd done it."

"Stop!" calls Celeste. "That's dangerous, you two.

The  is rusty. And you shouldn't

touch things that don't belong to you. Let's go on."

hatchet,
power saw,
pipe, log,
hand saw

After they all leave the clearing, the only sound is

that of a sharp-beaked  tapping for

insects in the bark of a tree. The children see a

beautiful large  with many-

colored feathers, but suddenly, there is a flash of red.

 "A !" cries Flora. "He'll catch it!

Quick, Pom, play your harmonica as loudly as you

can!" The pheasant, startled by the noise, flies away.

"It scarcely lost a single ," says Zephir

happily. The fox, annoyed and still hungry, goes

back to his burrow, hidden in a .

woodpecker,
pheasant,
fox,
feather,
stump

Babar has decided that they must stay together so

they won't get lost. Behind a big green 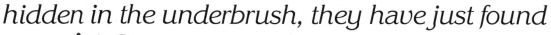 ,

hidden in the underbrush, they have just found

a  . The Old Lady exclaims, "Isn't

she pretty! What a lovely picture they make."

"Oh! look at the tiny  ," whispers Flora. "I've

never seen anything so sweet."

Then Pom says in a shaky voice, "Look! I can see

branches moving behind the 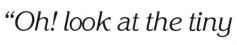 !"

"No , silly," says Arthur. "Those are the antlers of

the big  . He is watching the little one."

pine,
pine cone,
heather,
sweater,
beetle

While chasing after a , the children have

spotted a dead tree where the hive is located.

On it hangs a large bunch of  .

A loud grunting sound sends them into hiding.

"It's a big  !" they whisper, panic-

stricken. "Look!" murmurs Pom. "It's found the

honey, and behind the tree, there's a  !"

Suddenly, the huge honey thief stands up eight feet

tall! This frightens a  as well as the

children. "Let's get away before it sees us!" cries

Arthur, and they scatter into the woods.

bee,
mistletoe,
bear,
bear cub,
ferret

The little adventurers catch up with the rest of the

group at the side of a stream. Babar has thrown

a fallen  across the river to make

a bridge for the Old Lady.

Pom and Flora are building a  .

"You only know how to build dams," says Pom

to the  who is watching them curiously.

"That may be true," says Celeste, "but he doesn't

need a hatchet, a saw, a hammer, or a

to measure with." Lucky Arthur. He has found a

smooth, flat  for skipping on the water.

tree trunk,
raft,
beaver,
ball of string,
stone

"Picnicking here by the stream is a wonderful idea,"

says Celeste. She hands Babar a toasted

and asks, "Flora, will you please pass the napkins?"

Pom has a ripe and Zephir wants to

share it. Impatiently, he says, "Come on, Pom!"

"Hush! That 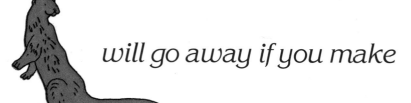 will go away if you make

too much noise," warns Arthur. "Isn't it funny how

it floats along with the  on its stomach?"

"It's lunchtime for everyone in the woods now,"

says Alexander. "Watch how quickly this hungry

blue  dives—it's like lightning."

sandwich,
tomato,
otter,
fish,
kingfisher

While Celeste, the Old Lady, and Babar sit and

drink their coffee, the children go off exploring.

Arthur discovers a big  in the mud,

and then another, and decides to follow them.

"A  !" cries Alexander excitedly.

"Look, it's the bear cub we saw before," whispers

Zephir. "He wants to play with that  ."

Suddenly, Flora gives a cry of alarm. "Look out!

It's a big  ! Help! Help!" she calls. The

children run, but it's the snake who's in danger:

High above the rocky cave, an  has seen it.

footprint, cave, toad, snake, eagle

The hikers are tired, and it is getting late, so they

decide to turn back. Suddenly, they are startled

to see a concealed steel  snap shut

on Babar's walking stick. He is very angry to see it:

"This  might have been caught!"

"And if it had been," says Flora, turning pale at the

idea, "what would the  have done?"

Zephir turns around quickly to see the boars and

slips on some rocks covered with green  .

"Look out!" he cries. "Another wild beast!"

"It's only a  ," says Alexander.

trap,
wild boar,
baby boar,
moss,
badger

Suddenly, the weather begins to grow stormy.

The wind blows hard, and a big  darkens the sky. Raindrops are falling fast.

"I've found the little  we made," says

Zephir. "We can take shelter there! Hurry up!" But

a tall  has come down across the path.

"Oh, dear," exclaims Arthur, "this is a shame.

The 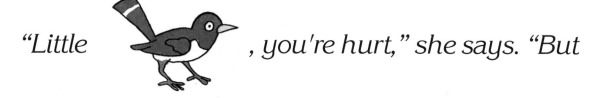 has fallen, and the eggs are smashed."

Flora rescues a striped magpie from the empty nest.

"Little , you're hurt," she says. "But

don't worry. We'll fix your broken wing."

cloud, hut,
tree limb,
nest, bird

The hut is so small that they are very crowded.

Zephir sees a young 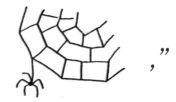 stealing some eggs,

but he doesn't want kind-hearted Flora to notice.

"I'm sitting too close to this big old  ,"

he says. "Please move over a bit, Flora."

"Don't disturb Papa's  please, Zephir,"

whispers Flora. "It's the new nest for my magpie."

Suddenly, a  splits the grey sky, followed

by a great clap of thunder. To distract the children,

Babar finds a big in his pocket.

"Here's something to cheer us up," he laughs.

weasel, spider web, cap, lightning bolt, chocolate bar

The sun is out again, with a beautiful .

Now the hikers are at the woods' edge, near home.

Oh! A 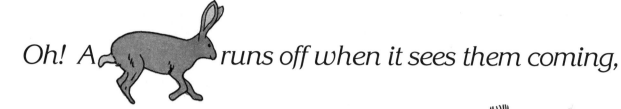 runs off when it sees them coming,

leaving behind its dinner—a tasty .

"I bet you aren't brave enough to touch this big

prickly ," says Pom to Alexander.

"We must get home soon," says Babar. "It's late."

But everyone is taking his time. "Wait," says Flora,

"I must give a handful of grass to the brown ."

"I've found something for dinner," says Zephir. "We

can share this big mushroom when we get home."

rainbow, hare,
dandelion,
nettle, pony

After a hot bath, the children bring their day's

treasures to the big 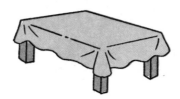 in the kitchen.

Arthur is so hungry that he eats before dinner:

a . Zephir wants to have one too, but—

"Ouch!" he yells, shaking his hand. "I pinched

my finger with the  . It hurts!"

"Instead of beginning with dessert, you two,"

scolds Celeste, shaking a  on top of the

stove, "someone should set the table. The

mushroom omelet needs only a little  to

make it even better. Dinner's ready!"

table,
walnut,
nutcracker,
frying pan,
parsley

Now all the children are making souvenirs

of their beautiful day in the forest. Arthur puts

dried leaves in a  . The others paint.

"It's hard to get the colors right," sighs Alexander.

"Your  , Zephir—the paint is dripping!"

calls Celeste. "And please let me get you a glass of

water: Don't suck on the end of your  !"

"I wouldn't do anything that foolish," says Pom;

"besides, I'm using a  . It's better."

"Soon," Flora says to the magpie, "you can leave the

 . We'll take you back to the forest."

notebook,
palette,
paintbrush,
pencil,
cage